A Rookie reader®

Field Day

Written by Melanie Davis Jones
Illustrated by Albert Molnar

Children's Press®
A Division of Scholastic Inc.
New York • Toronto • London • Auckland • Sydney
Mexico City • New Delhi • Hong Kong
Danbury, Connecticut

[BEGINNING READER]
JONES

To Teresa Sowell, Greg Davis, Ed Blount,
and to P.E. teachers everywhere
—M.D.J.

To my children, Sabrina, Tyler, and Baby-on-the-Way,
and my wife, Danica
—A.M.

Reading Consultants

Linda Cornwell
Literacy Specialist

Katharine A. Kane
Education Consultant
(Retired, San Diego County Office of Education
and San Diego State University)

Library of Congress Cataloging-in-Publication Data

Jones, Melanie Davis.
 Field day / written by Melanie Davis Jones ; illustrated by Albert
Molnar.
   p. cm. – (Rookie reader)
Summary: Children have a wonderful time participating in the various
activities of their school's field day.
 ISBN 0-516-22880-3 (lib. bdg.)   0-516-27772-3 (pbk.)
 [1. Racing–Fiction. 2. Contests–Fiction. 3. Schools–Fiction.] I.
Molnar, Albert, ill. II. Title. III. Series.
 PZ7.J 235Fi 2003
 [E]—dc21

                              2003003895

Running fast
Walking slowly

On your mark.

Mom and Dad
smiling proud.

Clapping hands.
Cheering crowd.

Egg and spoon.

13

Relay races.

Drinks and snacks.

Painted faces.

Hula hoop.

Balloon pop.

Toss the ball.

Time to stop!

Way to go.
Hip, hip, hooray!

What a great field day!

Word List (45 words)

a	faces	mark	smiling
and	fast	Mom	snacks
ball	field	on	spoon
balloon	get	painted	stop
cheering	go	pop	the
clapping	great	proud	time
crowd	hands	races	to
Dad	hip	relay	toss
day	hoop	running	walking
drinks	hooray	set	way
egg	hula	slow	what
			your

About the Author

As an elementary school teacher, Melanie Davis Jones has participated in many field day events throughout the years. Her favorite events are the egg and spoon relay and the balloon pop. When field day is over, she likes to go home and take a long nap. Mrs. Jones lives in Georgia with her husband and three sons.

About the Illustrator

Albert Molnar is an award-winning illustrator from Ottawa, Ontario, Canada. He has been illustrating children's books for thirteen years. In his spare time, he enjoys making supper, changing diapers, golfing, and spending time with his children, Sabrina and Tyler, and wife, Danica.